Sticker Fun
Horses and
Unicorns

Silver Dolphin

The Enchanted Forest

Welcome to the Enchanted Forest!
Here horses and unicorns come to play.
Add more horse and unicorn friends
to the happy scene.

Over the Rainbow

Horses and unicorns must cross the Rainbow
Bridge to reach the Enchanted Forest.
Add fluttering fairy friends
to the scene.

Forest Friends

Unicorns are not the only magical creatures that live and play in the Enchanted Forest. Add more forest friends to the scene.

Magical Candy Orchard

Horses and unicorns love sweet treats! Add more candy delights for the friends to eat.

Moonlit Pony Parade

Every year there is a fabulous pony parade through the Enchanted Forest. Add stickers to complete the magical moonlit procession.

At the Races

Horses and unicorns enjoy racing against their friends! Who will win this race around the Enchanted Forest track?

Midsummer Ball

On the longest day of the year, the unicorns hold a magnificent midsummer ball. Manes are colored and hooves are painted for this magical celebration. Add some more fabulous guests to the ballroom.

Cute Creatures

Unicorns help protect the other animals who live in the Enchanted Forest. Find some more forest animals to complete the friendly scene.

Winter Wonderland

It's a magical moonlit night and the horses and unicorns are playing in a snowy field. Add more fantastic beasts to the wintry scene.

Fable Stables

At night, the horses like to relax in their stables. Give them buckets of food and some blankets to keep them warm.

Pretty Unicorns

Unicorns love to wear sparkling jewels and colorful flowers in their manes. Add more jewels and flowers to the unicorns.

Wild Berry Harvest

Horses and unicorns love eating wild berries!
Add more berries for the happy horses,
unicorns, and fairies to collect.

Unicorn Dressage Trials

It's the day of the riderless dressage championship and unicorns from far and wide have come to compete. Add more unicorns to the stadium scene.

Unicorn Cross-Country Trials

Cross-country trials are tough—there are lots of tricky obstacles! Add more obstacles and unicorns to the course.

Unicorn Show Jumping Trials

It's the final event of the unicorn trials. Who will win the show jumping event and be crowned champion? Add some jumping unicorns for the crowd to cheer on.

Motherly Love

Some of the unicorns have just given birth to their very first foals! Add more foals next to their proud mothers in this springtime scene.

Pegasus

Pegasus is the only winged horse in the Enchanted Forest. He loves to swoop in and out of the clouds with his hippogriff friends. Add more hippogriffs to the sky scene.

Hide-and-Seek

Horses and unicorns love to play hide-and-seek!
Hide more horses and unicorns so they
are difficult to spot.

Magical Maze

Some parts of the Enchanted Forest are just like a maze! Fill the forest with horses and unicorns trying to reach their grazing spot.

Mountain Picnic

Close to the tallest mountains in the Enchanted Forest, there is a perfect place for horses and unicorns to enjoy a picnic! Add more horses and unicorns to the picnic.

Mermaid Lagoon

Mermaids and seahorses visit with the horses and unicorns as they stop to drink water at Mystic Lagoon. Finish the happy scene.

Moon Dance

Whenever there is a full moon, the unicorns travel deep into the Enchanted Forest to the unicorn castle for a special midnight moon dance. Add a moon, stars, fairies, and lanterns to the scene!

A Unicorn Wedding

These unicorns are getting married!
Finish the happy scene so the
couple can celebrate in style!

Good Neigh-bors!

Horses and unicorns love to be groomed!
Their fairy neighbors keep their manes and tails
tangle-free. Add fairies to groom the unicorn!